Avocado Asks

For my mum,
who never asks what I am.
M. A.

ORCHARD BOOKS

First published in Great Britain in 2020 by The Watts Publishing Group

1 3 5 7 9 10 8 6 4 2

Text and illustrations © Momoko Abe 2020

The moral rights of the author-illustrator have been asserted.

A CIP catalogue record for this book is available from the British Library.

HB ISBN 978 1 40835 822 1
PB ISBN 978 1 40835 823 8

Printed and bound in China

Orchard Books
An imprint of Hachette Children's Group
Part of The Watts Publishing Group Limited
Carmelite House, 50 Victoria Embankment, London EC4Y 0DZ

An Hachette UK Company
www.hachette.co.uk
www.hachettechildrens.co.uk

Avocado Asks

What am I?

by Momoko Abe

ORCHARD

Avocado was feeling just fine in the
fruit and vegetable aisle of the supermarket.

Life was pretty simple. No doubts.
No questions. No confusion . . .

until one day a small
customer pointed
and asked:

"Mum . . .

Suddenly Avocado's world
turned upside down.

Fruit?

Vegetable?

Avocado didn't know
the answer either.

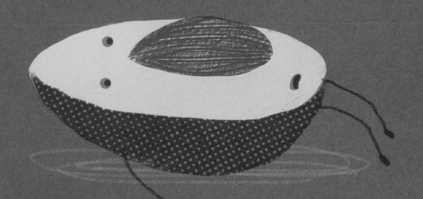

So Avocado
asked the vegetables:
"Am I a vegetable?"

The vegetables seemed muddled at first,
but then the cabbages said, "You're not leafy like us."
"And you're not crunchy like us," the carrots cut in.
"And vegetables don't have a big stone in the middle,
like you do," grumbled the potatoes.

"So . . .

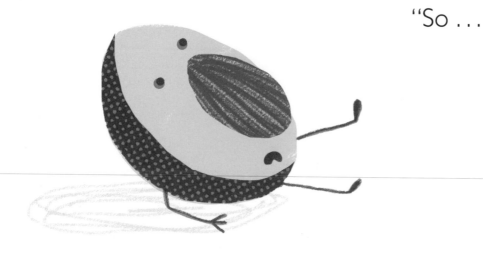

You're NOT a VEGETABLE!

OK, I must be a fruit then,
thought Avocado.

So Avocado asked the fruits:
"Am I a fruit?"

"You're not sweet and juicy
like us," said the pears.
"No one would eat you as
dessert," giggled the bananas.
"You belong in a salad –
but NOT a fruit salad,"
chuckled the peaches.

Avocado's insides felt like
they were turning to guacamole.

"I don't belong with the
vegetables OR the fruit!

There must be somewhere
I can feel at home . . .

"But where?"

"I'm pretty sure I'm not a herb . . .

BASIL CHIVES THYME

or a sausage.

GARDEN PEAS GARDEN PEAS GARDEN PEAS GARDE

KIDNEY BEANS KIDNEY BEANS KIDNEY BEANS KIDNEY BEANS

I know I'm not a tinned pea or a bean."

SWEETCORN SWEETCORN SWEETCORN SWEETCORN SWEETCORN

PLUM TOMATO PLUM TOMATO PLUM TOMATO PLUM TOMATO PLUM TOMATO PLU

Avocado came to the fish counter.
With their fins and scales, the fish looked
very different. But it was worth a try.

"Am I a fish?"

"Don't be silly, avocados can't
swim," said the fish coldly.

You're NOT a
FISH!

FRESH MACKEREL

SEASONAL SCALLOPS

But what about the cheeses?
Some of them were ROUND, like Avocado.
Some of them had HARD SKIN on the outside too.

"Am I a cheese?" asked Avocado.

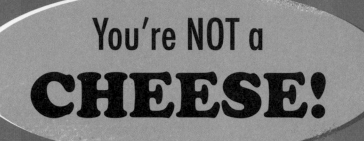

You're NOT a
CHEESE!

emmental

brie

They smell a lot like feet, thought Avocado.
I'm rather glad I'm not a cheese. Maybe I'm an ...

Avocado was more confused than ever.
"I'm not a fruit, a vegetable, a fish, a cheese or an egg.

SO WHAT AM I?"

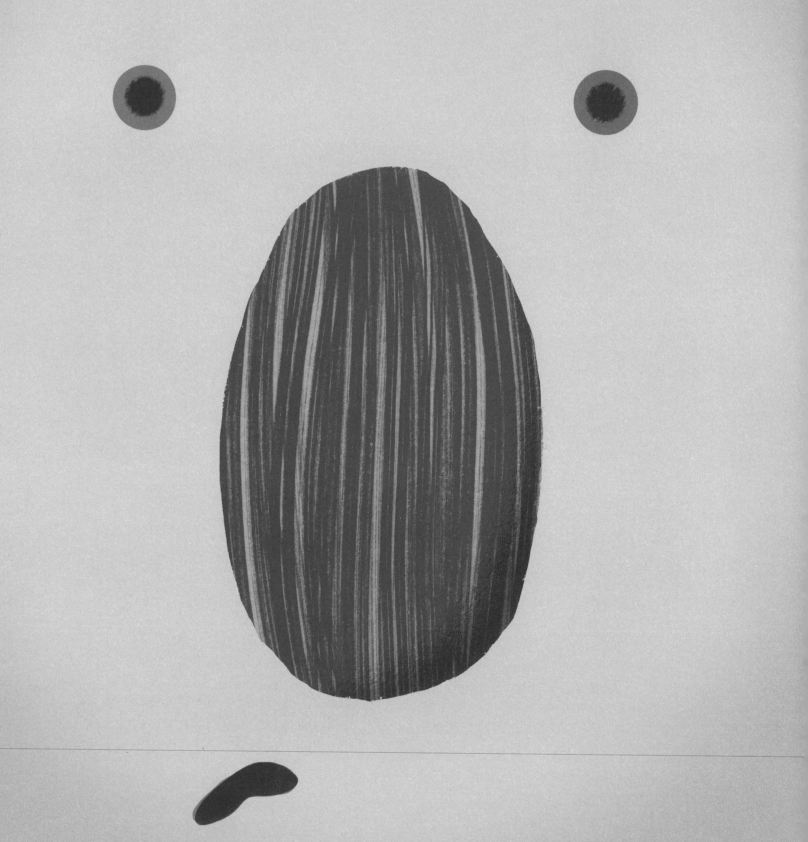

Far from the fruit and vegetable section,
Avocado was feeling lost and lonely.

And that was when
Avocado heard . . .

"Cheer up, *amigo*!" said Tomato.
"You don't know what you are?
So what! Don't stew in your
own juices. I'm a fruit but no
one believes me.

And I. Don't. Care.

"Because I'm tasty
hot or cold.

I make splendid salads
and superb soup.

People love me
on pizza ...

and adore me
with pasta.

TOMATO
KETCHUP

And they can't
get enough
of my ketchup!

And you, Avocado ...

"You're the star of any salad.

You're terrific on toast, and tremendous in tacos.

You're scrumptious
in sushi . . .

and your guacamole
is so delicious that
the other fruit and
vegetables go green
with envy."

"Who cares what we are, when **we're simply AMAZING!"**

said Tomato.

It was true. They could just be themselves and that was enough. Suddenly Avocado didn't feel lost and lonely any more.

And that was when they heard,

Excuse me . . .

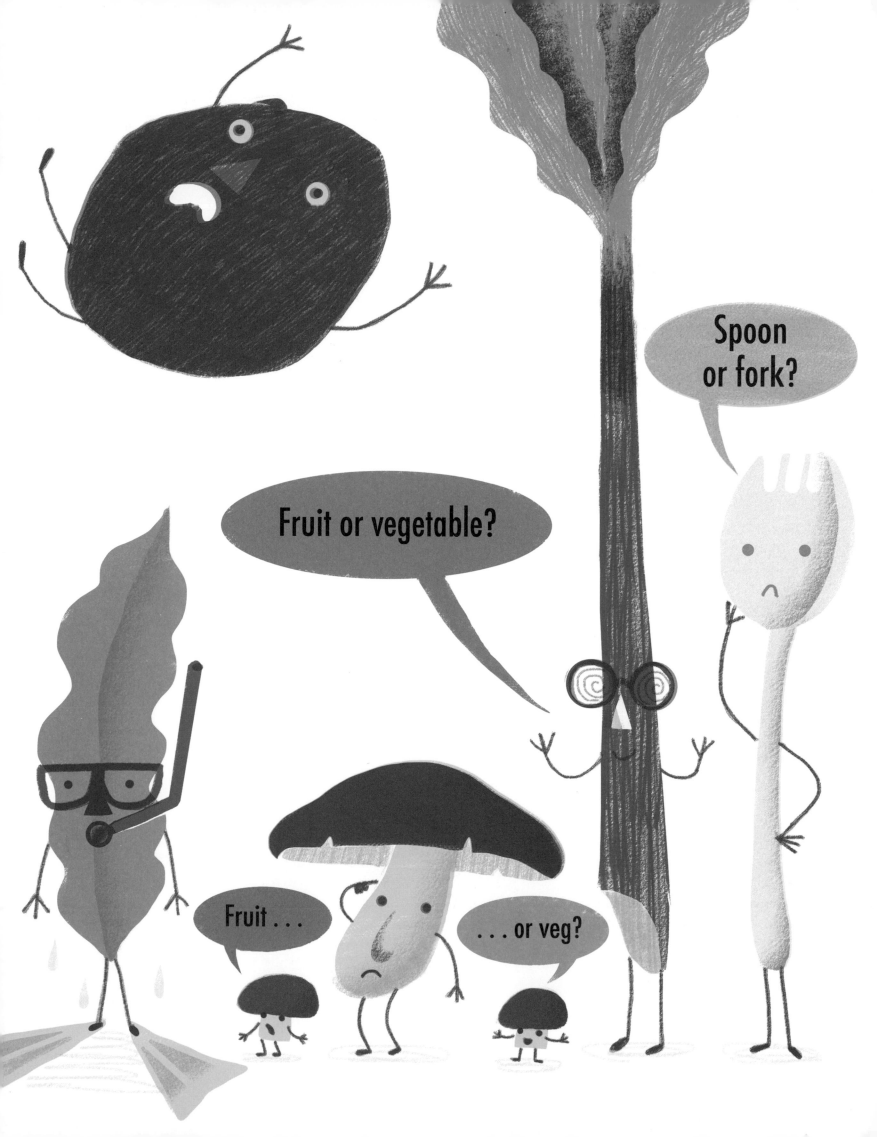

The end.